Meg and Ted

by Katie Woolley and Kelly Caswell

W
FRANKLIN WATTS

LONDON•SYDNEY

Meg was shopping
with Mum.

Ted helped, too.

2

3

Meg was dusting
with Dad.

Ted helped, too.

Meg was digging
with Gran.

Ted helped, too.

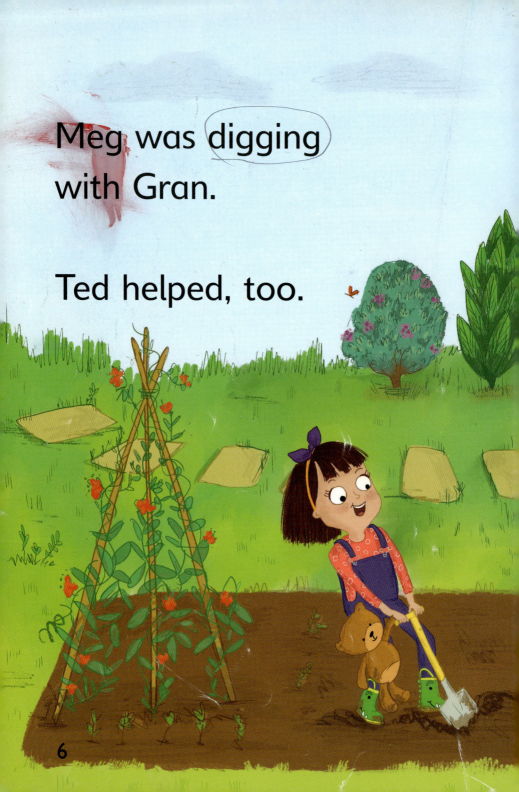

Meg was cleaning
with Grandad.

Ted helped, too.

Meg was cooking
with Dad.

Ted helped, too.

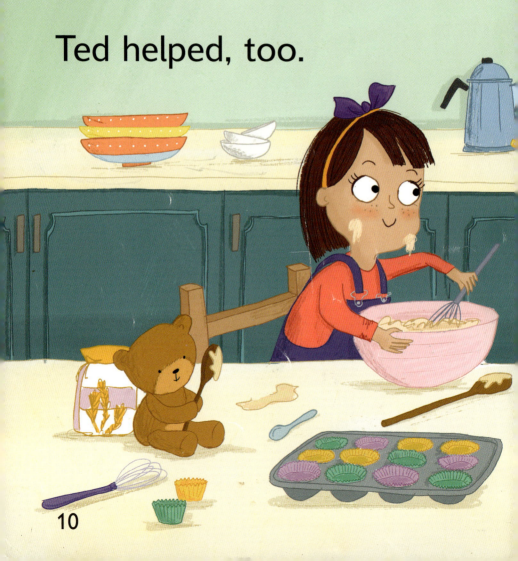

11

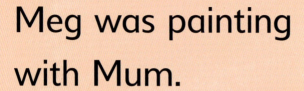

Meg was painting
with Mum.

Ted helped, too.

13

Meg was washing
with Gran.

Ted helped, too.

15

Meg was reading
with Grandad.

Ted helped, too.

17

Meg was sleeping
with Ted.

Ted was sleeping, too.

18

Story trail

Start

Start at the beginning of the story trail. Ask your child to retell the story in their own words, pointing to each picture in turn to recall the sequence of events.

Independent Reading

This series is designed to provide an opportunity for your child to read on their own. These notes are written for you to help your child choose a book and to read it independently.

In school, your child's teacher will often be using reading books which have been banded to support the process of learning to read. Use the book band colour your child is reading in school to help you make a good choice. *Meg and Ted* is a good choice for children reading at Red Band in their classroom to read independently.

The aim of independent reading is to read this book with ease, so that your child enjoys the story and relates it to their own experiences.

About the book

Meg likes to help her family in whatever they are doing— and she never goes anywhere without her trusted bear, Ted, who also likes to help!

Before reading

Help your child to learn how to make good choices by asking: "Why did you choose this book? Why do you think you will enjoy it?" Support your child to think about what they already know about the story context. Look at the cover together and ask: "What do you think the story will be about?" Read the title aloud and ask: "How do you think Meg feels about her teddy bear?"

Remind your child that they can try to sound out the letters to make a word if they get stuck.

Decide together whether your child will read the story independently or read it aloud to you. When books are short, as at Red Band, your child may wish to do both!

During reading

If reading aloud, support your child if they hesitate or ask for help by telling the word. Remind your child of what they know and what they can do independently.

If reading to themselves, remind your child that they can come and ask for your help if stuck.

After reading

Support comprehension by asking your child to tell you about the story. Use the story trail to encourage your child to retell the story in the right sequence, in their own words.

Give your child a chance to respond to the story: "Did you have a favourite part? What task would you help someone to do?"

Help your child think about the messages in the book that go beyond the story and ask: "Why does Meg share her tasks with Ted?" "Why do you think Meg likes to help?"

Extending learning

Help your child extend the story structure by using the same sentence pattern and adding some more elements. For example, Josh is tidying up his toys. Max (the pet dog) helps Josh, too.

On a few of the pages, check your child can finger point accurately by asking them to show you how they kept their place in the print by tracking from word to word.

Help your child to use letter information by asking them to find the interest word on each page by using the first letter. For example: "Which word is 'cooking'? How did you know it was that word?"

Franklin Watts
First published in Great Britain in 2019
by The Watts Publishing Group

Copyright © The Watts Publishing Group 2019

Series Editors: Jackie Hamley and Melanie Palmer
Series Advisors: Dr Sue Bodman and Glen Franklin
Series Designer: Peter Scoulding

A CIP catalogue record for this book is
available from the British Library.

ISBN 978 1 4451 6768 8 (hbk)
ISBN 978 1 4451 6770 1 (pbk)
ISBN 978 1 4451 6769 5 (library ebook)

Printed in China

Franklin Watts
An imprint of
Hachette Children's Group
Part of The Watts Publishing Group
Carmelite House
50 Victoria Embankment
London EC4Y 0DZ

An Hachette UK Company
www.hachette.co.uk

www.franklinwatts.co.uk